THE STRANGE
CASE OF DR JEKYLL
AND MR HYDE

THE STRANGE CASE OF DR JEKYLL AND MR HYDE

Robert Louis Stevenson

An imprint of Om Books International

First published in 2015

An imprint of Om Books International

Corporate & Editorial Office
A-12, Sector 64, Noida 201 301
Uttar Pradesh, India
Phone: +91 120 477 4100
Email: editorial@ombooks.com
Website: www.ombooksinternational.com

Sales Office
107, Ansari Road, Darya Ganj
New Delhi 110 002, India
Phone: +91 11 4000 9000, 2326 3363, 2326 5303
Fax: +91 11 2327 8091
Email: sales@ombooks.com
Website: www.ombooks.com

ISBN: 978-93-84225-51-3

Printed in India

10 9 8 7 6 5 4 3 2 1

Contents

Chapter One

The Story of the Door

Mr Utterson the lawyer was a man with a rugged face never lighted by a smile; cold, scanty and embarrassed in conversation; backward in expressing his feelings; lean, long, dusty, dreary and yet somehow lovable. At friendly meetings, and when the wine was to his taste, something very human shone forth from his eyes. He was strict with himself; drank gin when he was alone to subdue his taste for wines, and despite enjoying the theatre, had not treated himself to one for twenty years. But he was tolerant; when faced with the misdeeds of others, he found himself wondering at the causes prompting such

and silently empathising with them rather than judging them. Because of his rare quality of not judging nor changing his behaviour towards immoral men, he frequently ended up being the only reputable acquaintance and the last good influence in the lives of such men.

His friends were those of his own blood or those whom he had known the longest; his affections, like ivy, were the growth of time, they were not chosen on merit. The bond that united him to Mr Richard Enfield, his distant cousin and the well-known man about town, was like this. It was a nut to crack for many, what these two could see in each other, or what subject they could find in common. Those who encountered them in their Sunday walks reported that they said nothing to each other, looked singularly dull and would hail with obvious relief the appearance of a friend. For all that, the two men never missed these weekly excursions. They even resisted the calls of business and other pleasurable gatherings so that they might enjoy these walks uninterrupted.

It was on one of these rambles that they chanced to find themselves in a bystreet in a busy quarter of London. The street was small and quiet, but trade thrived on it on weekdays. The inhabitants were all doing well, it seemed and all hoping to do better still; the shop fronts along the thoroughfare had an air of invitation, like rows of smiling saleswomen. Even on Sundays, when it was stripped of its more florid charms and lay comparatively empty, the street shone out in contrast to its dingy neighbourhood, like a fire in a forest— its freshly painted shutters, well-polished brasses, and general air of cleanliness and gaiety instantly caught and pleased the eye of the passenger.

Two doors from one corner, on the left hand going east, the line was broken by a court, and just at that point, a certain sinister two-storeyed, building thrust forward its gable on the street. There was nothing but a door on the lower storey and a blind forehead of discoloured wall on the upper; it bore the unmistakable marks of

of prolonged and sordid negligence. The door had neither bell nor knocker, and was blistered and discoloured. Tramps used to slouch into its dark, secluded spots and struck matches on the panels; a schoolboy had tried his knife skills on the mouldings; for years, no one had driven away these random visitors or repaired their ravages.

Mr Enfield paused in front of the entry, lifted up his cane and pointed.

"Did you ever notice that door?" he asked, "it is connected in my mind with a very odd story."

"Indeed?" asked Mr Utterson, with a slight change of voice, "and what was that?"

"Well, it was this way," replied Mr Enfield, "I was coming home from some place at the end of the world, at about three o'clock on a black winter morning. I passed through a part of town where there was literally nothing to be seen but lamps. Street after street and all the folks asleep—street after street, all lighted up as if for a procession and all as empty as a church—till at last I got into that state of mind when a man listens and listens and

begins to long for the sight of something human. All at once, I saw two figures: one a little man stumping along briskly and the other a girl of maybe eight or ten who was running as hard as she could. Well, sir, the two ran into one another at the corner, and then came the horrible part for the man trampled calmly over the child's body and left her screaming on the ground. It was horrible to see. It wasn't like a man; it was like Juggernaut.

"I shouted, ran up to the man, collared him and brought him back to the group which had collected around the screaming child. He was perfectly cool and unresisting, but gave me a look so ugly that it brought out the sweat on me. The people who had crowded around were the girl's own family and pretty soon, the doctor arrived. The child was found to be not so much hurt as frightened. But curiously, all of us seemed to have taken a loathing to the gentleman at first sight. I never saw a circle of such hateful faces and there was the man in the middle, with a kind of black, sneering coolness—frightened too, I could see

that—but carrying it off well. The women of the family looked as wild as the mythical harpies with the desire to attack him. We told him that if he didn't pay the damages, we could and would make such a scandal out of this, that his name would stink from one end of London to the other.

'If you choose to make profit out of this accident,' said he, 'I'm naturally helpless. A gentleman would of course wish to avoid a scene. Name your figure.'

"Well, we asked him for a hundred pounds for the child's family. The next thing was to get the money and where do you think he took us? That place with the door. He whipped out a key, went in and returned with ten pounds in gold and a cheque for the balance on Coutts's, drawn payable to bearer and signed with a name that I can't mention—it was a name very well known and often seen in print. I doubted if the signature was genuine.

'Set your mind at rest,' said he sneeringly, 'I will stay with you till the banks open and cash the cheque myself.'

"And so all of us passed the rest of the night in my chambers. The next day after breakfast we went to the bank. I deposited the cheque myself. It was genuine."

"Tut-tut," said Mr Utterson.

"This man was a fellow that nobody would want to associate with, a really evil-looking man," continued Mr Enfield, "and the person in whose name the cheque was drawn was a wealthy and celebrated altruist. Blackmail, I suppose; an honest man paying through the nose for some of the capers of his youth. Consequently, Blackmail House is what I call that place with the door," and he fell into deep thought.

"And you don't know if the drawer of the cheque lives there?" asked Mr Utterson rather suddenly.

"No, he lives in some square or the other," said Mr Enfield. "And no, I never asked him about this. It was too delicate a matter. I feel very strongly about putting questions. You start a question, and it's like throwing a stone from

the top of a hill; away the stone goes, startling others, and presently some bland old bird (the last you would have thought of) is knocked on the head in his own back garden and the family have to change their name. No, sir, I make it a rule of mine: the more it looks like Queer Street, the less I ask."

"A very good rule, too," said Mr Utterson.

"But I have studied the place for myself," continued Mr Enfield. "It seems scarcely like a house. There is no other door, and nobody goes in or out of that but the gentleman of my adventure, and that too rarely. The windows on the first floor are always shut but they're clean. And then there is a chimney which is generally smoking, so somebody must live there."

The pair walked on again in silence and then Mr Utterson said, "Enfield, that's a good rule of yours. But still, I want to ask the name of the man who walked over the child."

"Well," said Mr Enfield, "I can't see what harm it would do. He was a man called Hyde."

"Hmm," said Mr Utterson. "What did he look like?"

"He is not easy to describe," said Enfield. "There is something wrong with his appearance; something displeasing, something downright repulsive. I never saw a man I so disliked, and yet I scarcely know why. He gives a strong feeling of deformity though I can't specify where. He's an extraordinary-looking man, and yet I really can name nothing out of the ordinary. No, sir; I can't describe him. And it's not because I don't remember for I can visualise him even now, at this moment."

Mr Utterson again walked in silence, obviously considering.

"You're sure he used a key?" he inquired at last.

"My dear sir..." began Mr Enfield, surprised out of himself.

"Yes, I know," said Mr Utterson; "I may appear too curious, but the fact is if I do not ask you the name of the other party, it's because I know it already."

"You might have warned me," said the other, a little sullenly. "Yes, the fellow had a key and what's more, he still has it. I saw him use it, less than a week ago."

Mr Utterson sighed deeply but did not say anything.

"I'm ashamed of my long tongue," said Mr Enfield after a while. "Let's agree never to refer to this again."

"Of course, Richard," said the lawyer.

Chapter Two

The Search for Mr Hyde

That evening Mr Utterson returned to his bachelor house in sombre spirits and sat down to dinner without relish. It was his Sunday custom to sit close by the fire after his meal with a volume of some dry theological text on his reading desk, until the neighbouring church clock rang out the hour of twelve, when he would go soberly and gratefully to bed.

On this night, however, as soon as he had finished his meal, he went to his study. There he opened his safe, took out a document labelled on the envelope as Dr Jekyll's Will and sat down to study its contents, his brow clouded.

It was written in Dr Jekyll's hand. The will was holograph for Mr Utterson, though he had taken charge of it after its completion, had refused to lend the least assistance in the making of it. It stated that, in case of the death of Henry Jekyll, all his possessions were to pass into the hands of his "friend and benefactor Edward Hyde", but that in case of Dr Jekyll's "disappearance or unexplained absence for any period exceeding three calendar months," the said Edward Hyde should step into the said Henry Jekyll's shoes without further delay, free from any obligations beyond the payment of a few small sums to the members of the doctor's household.

This document had long been the lawyer's eyesore. It offended him both as a lawyer and as a lover of sanity. It was bad that he knew nothing of the person. It was worse now; he had found out that Mr Hyde had bad attributes; and out of the shifting, insubstantial mists that had so long puzzled him, there leaped up the sudden, definite image of a demon.

"I thought it was madness," he said, as he replaced the obnoxious paper in the safe, "and now I begin to fear it is disgrace."

With that he blew out his candle, put on a great-coat and set forth in the direction of Cavendish Square, that citadel of medicine, where his friend, the great Dr Lanyon lived. *If anyone knows, it will be Lanyon*, he thought.

The solemn butler who knew him well welcomed him; without delay, he was ushered directly to the dining room where Dr Lanyon sat alone with his wine. He was a hearty, healthy, dapper, red-faced gentleman with a boisterous manner. At the sight of Mr Utterson, he sprang up from his chair and welcomed him effusively. Though somewhat theatrical to the eye, this geniality was the way of the man, and it sprang from genuine feeling—for these two were old friends from school and college, men who respected each other and thoroughly enjoyed each other's company.

After a little rambling talk, the lawyer started upon the subject which pre-occupied his mind so disagreeably.

"I suppose, Lanyon," said he "you and I must be the two oldest friends that Henry Jekyll has?"

"I suppose we are," replied Dr Lanyon. "But I see little of him now."

"Indeed?" said Utterson. "I thought you had a bond of common interest."

"We had," was the reply. "But it is more than ten years since Henry Jekyll became too fanciful for me. He began to go wrong, wrong in mind; and though of course I continue to take an interest in him for old time's sake, as they say, I see very little of him. Such unscientific balderdash," added the doctor, suddenly flushing purple.

This little show of temper relieved Mr Utterson somewhat. *They've only differed on some scientific point, it's nothing worse than that!* he thought.

"Did you ever come across a protégé of his— one Hyde?" he asked.

"Hyde?" repeated Lanyon. "No. Never heard of him."

The meeting shed no further light on the mysterious identity of Mr Hyde. All night, and until the wee hours of the morning the lawyer tossed to and fro on his great, dark bed. His mind was filled with questions.

Hitherto the problem had touched him on the intellectual side alone, but now his imagination also was engaged, or rather enslaved. Mr Enfield's tale went by before his mind in a scroll of lighted pictures. He saw the great field of lamps of a nocturnal city; then of the figure of a man walking swiftly; then of a child running; then they met, and that human Juggernaut trod the child down and passed on regardless of her screams. He also saw a room in a rich house, where his friend lay asleep, pleasantly dreaming and smiling; and then the door of that room would be opened, the curtains of the bed plucked apart, and lo! There would be a figure who had infinite power over his friend, and whose bidding he must follow. This figure haunted the lawyer all night, and even if at any time he dozed, he saw

it glide more stealthily through sleeping houses, or move swiftly and still more swiftly, his speed verging on dizziness, through the labyrinths of the lamp-lighted city, and at every street corner crush a child and leave her screaming. And still the figure was unrecognizable.

And thus a singularly strong, almost an inordinate curiosity grew in the lawyer's mind to see the features of the real Mr Hyde. If he could but see him once, he thought, the mystery would lighten and perhaps roll altogether away, as was the habit of mysterious things when well examined. He might see a reason for his friend's strange preference or bondage and perhaps even for the startling clause of the will.

From that time onwards, Mr Utterson began to haunt the door in the bystreet of the shops. In the morning before office hours, at noon when business was plenty and at night under the fogged city moon, at all hours, the lawyer was to be found on his chosen post.

If he be Mr Hyde I shall be Mr Seek he thought.

And at last his patience was rewarded. It was a fine dry night with frost in the air; the streets as clean as a ballroom floor; the lamps, unshaken by any wind, drawing a regular pattern of light and shadow. By ten o'clock, when the shops were closed, the bystreet became very solitary and, in spite of the low growl of London from all round, very silent. Small sounds carried far. The domestic sounds out of the houses were clearly audible, and the sound of the approach of any passenger preceded him by a long time. Mr Utterson had been some minutes at his post, when he was aware of an odd, light footstep drawing near. His attention had never before been so sharply and decisively arrested, and it was with a strong, superstitious premonition of success that he withdrew into the entry of the court.

The steps drew swiftly nearer and swelled out louder as they turned the end of the street. The man approaching was small, and the look

of him, even at that distance, repelled the observer. He made straight for the door, and as he came, he drew a key from his pocket like one approaching home.

Mr Utterson stepped out and touched him on the shoulder as he passed. "Mr Hyde, I think?"

Mr Hyde shrank back with a hissing intake of the breath. But his fear was only momentary; and though he did not look the lawyer in the face, he answered coolly enough, "That is my name. What do you want?"

"I see you're going in," replied the lawyer. "I am an old friend of Dr Jekyll's — Mr Utterson of Gaunt Street — you must have heard my name."

"Dr Jekyll is away from home," replied Mr Hyde.

And then suddenly, but still without looking up he asked, "How did you know me?"

"Will you do me a favour first?" said Mr Utterson. "Will you let me see your face?"

Mr Hyde appeared to hesitate, and then suddenly faced him with an air of defiance. The pair stared at each other pretty fixedly for a few seconds.

"Now I shall know you again," said Mr Utterson. "It may be useful."

"Yes," said Mr Hyde, "it is well that we have met; this is my address."

And he gave a number of a street in Soho.

Good God! thought Mr Utterson, *is he thinking of the will*? But he kept his feelings to himself and only grunted in acknowledgment.

"And now," said the other, "How did you know me?"

"By description," was the reply.

"Whose description?"

"We have common friends," replied Mr Utterson.

"Common friends?" echoed Mr Hyde, a little hoarsely. "Who are they?"

"Jekyll, for instance," replied the lawyer.

"He never told you," cried Mr Hyde, with a flush of anger. "I do not think that you would have lied."

"Come," said Mr Utterson, "that is not the way to talk."

The other snarled aloud into a savage laugh and the next moment, with extraordinary quickness, he had unlocked the door and disappeared into the house.

Chapter Three

Dr Jekyll's Defence of his Mysterious Protégé

The lawyer stood there for a while after Mr Hyde's departure, looking the very picture of anxiousness. Then he began slowly to mount the street, pausing at every step or two and putting his hand to his brow like a man in mental perplexity. The problem he was debating was one of a class that is rarely solved.

Mr Hyde was pale and dwarfish, he gave an impression of being deformed, but without any nameable deformity, he had a displeasing smile, his attitude had been a sort of murderous mixture

of timidity and boldness, and he spoke with a husky, whispering and somewhat broken voice, but all of these together could not explain the unknown disgust, loathing and fear which he had aroused in Mr Utterson.

There must be something else. There is something more, if only I could find a name for it. God bless me, the man seems hardly human! Something degraded, primitive, or brutal, shall we say? Oh my poor old Harry Jekyll, if ever I read Satan's signature upon a face, it is on that of your new friend, thought the perplexed gentleman.

Round the corner from the bystreet, there was a square of ancient, handsome houses, now mostly decayed and let out as flats and chambers to all sorts of men. One house (second from the corner)was still occupied entirely; it still had a great air of wealth and comfort though it was now plunged in darkness except for the fanlight; at the door of this, Mr Utterson stopped and knocked. A well-dressed servant opened the door.

"Is Dr Jekyll at home, Poole?" asked the lawyer.

"I will see, Mr Utterson," said Poole, admitting the visitor, as he spoke, into a large, low-roofed, comfortable hall, paved with flags, warmed by a bright, open fire and furnished with costly oak cabinets.

"Will you wait here by the fire, sir? Or shall I give you a light in the dining room?" Poole asked.

"Here, thank you," said the lawyer, and he drew near and leaned on the tall fender.

This hall, in which he was now left alone, was his friend the doctor's favourite room, and Mr Utterson himself considered it to be the pleasantest room in London. But tonight, even as he stood there, he shuddered; the face of Hyde sat heavily on his memory; he felt (what was rare with him) a nausea and distaste for life. He seemed to read a menace even in the firelight flickering on the polished cabinets and the starting of shadows on the roof left him uneasy.

Poole presently returned to announce that Dr Jekyll was out.

"I saw Mr Hyde go in by the old dissecting-room door, Poole," he said. "Is that right, when Dr. Jekyll is from home?"

"Quite right, Mr Utterson, sir," replied the servant. "Mr Hyde has a key."

"Your master seems to put a great deal of trust in that young man, Poole," mused the other.

"Yes, sir, he does indeed," said Poole. "We all have orders to obey him."

"I do not think I ever met Mr Hyde?" asked Mr Utterson.

"Oh! dear no, sir. He never dines here," replied the butler. "We see very little of him on this side of the house; he mostly comes and goes by the laboratory."

"Well, goodnight, Poole."

"Goodnight, Mr Utterson."

The lawyer set out homeward with a very heavy heart. *Poor Harry Jekyll*, he thought, *I have doubts that he is in deep waters! He was wild when he was young–that was long ago to be sure – but yes – it*

must be that; the ghost of some old sin, the cancer of some hidden disgrace: punishment coming limping belatedly, pede claudo, years after one has forgotten and forgiven oneself.

And the lawyer, scared by the thought, brooded a while on his own past, groping in all the corners of memory if by chance some Jack-in-the-Box of an old sin should leap out. His past was fairly blameless yet he was humbled by the many ill things he thought he had done, and sobered and made grateful by the many he had avoided. In the process, he conceived a spark of hope.

This Master Hyde must have secrets of his own; black secrets, by the look of him; secrets compared to which poor Jekyll's worst would be like sunshine, thought he. *Things cannot continue as they are. It turns me cold to think of this creature tormenting Harry! And if this Hyde suspects the existence of the will, he may grow impatient to inherit and dispose of Harry altogether! I must intervene, if Jekyll will only let me.*

"If Jekyll will only let me," he repeated. Once more he saw before his mind's eye the strange clauses of the will.

A fortnight later, Dr Jekyll gave one of his pleasant dinners to some of his old friends, all intelligent, reputable men and all judges of good wine. Mr Utterson managed to remain behind after the others had departed. This was nothing new, but a thing that had happened many times before. Where Utterson was liked, he was liked well. After the light-hearted and the loose-tongued had left, the hosts loved to detain the dry lawyer; they liked to enjoy for a while his unobtrusive company, sobering their minds in the man's rich silence after the strain of gaiety. And thus now Dr Jekyll and his old friend were left behind.

Dr Jekyll was a large, well-made, smooth-faced man of fifty, a hint of slyness in his demeanor perhaps, but also with every mark of capability and kindness. It was apparent that

he cherished a sincere and warm affection for Mr Utterson.

"I've been wanting to speak to you, Jekyll," began the latter. "You know that will of yours?"

It was obvious that the topic was distasteful but the doctor carried it off gaily.

"My poor Utterson," said he, "I never saw a man so distressed as you were by my will unless I consider that obsessive Lanyon's distress at what he called my scientific defection. Oh, I know he's a good fellow — you needn't frown — an excellent fellow, and I always mean to see more of him, but he is ignorant. I was never more disappointed in any man than Lanyon."

"You know I never approved of it," pursued Utterson, ruthlessly disregarding his friend's attempt at changing the topic.

"My will? Yes, certainly, I know that," said the doctor, a little sharply. "You have told me so."

"Well, I will repeat my warning," said

the lawyer. "I recently learnt something of young Hyde."

The large handsome face of Dr Jekyll grew pale to the very lips, and his eyes grew dark. "I don't care to hear more," said he. "I thought we had agreed to drop this subject."

"What I heard was terrible," said Mr Utterson.

"It cannot change anything. You don't understand my position," said the doctor, rather incoherently. "I'm painfully situated, Utterson; my position is very strange — a very strange one. It cannot be mended by talking."

"Jekyll," said Utterson, "you know me. I'm a man to be trusted. Tell me every thing and I will spare no effort to get you out of it."

"Utterson," said the doctor, "this is downright good of you, and I cannot find the words to thank you. I believe you fully; I would trust you before any man alive, yes, before myself, if I could make the choice, but indeed it isn't what you fancy; it is not so bad as that; and just to put your good heart at rest, I will tell you one thing: the moment I choose, I can be rid of Hyde. And I will just add one little word, Utterson, that I'm sure you'll take in the right spirit: this is a private matter, and I beg you not to raise it again."

Mr Utterson reflected a little, looking in the fire.

"But since we have touched upon this business, and for the last time I hope," continued the doctor, "there is one point I would like you to understand. I know you have seen him; he told me so and I fear he was rude. But, I do sincerely take a great, a very great interest in that young man and if I'm taken away, Utterson, I wish you to promise me that you will see to it that he gets his rights. You would, if you knew all, and it would take a weight off my mind if you promise."

"I can't pretend that I shall ever like him," said the lawyer.

"I don't ask that," pleaded Jekyll, laying his hand upon the other's arm, "I'm only asking you to help him for my sake, when I'm no longer here."

Mr Utterson heaved a sigh.

"I promise," said he.

Chapter Four

The Carew Murder Case

Nearly a year later, in the month of October, 18—, London was startled by a crime of singular ferocity. It was made all the more notable by the high position of the victim. The details were few and startling. A maidservant living alone in a house not far from the river, had gone upstairs to bed about eleven. The night was cloudless, and the lane overlooked by the maid was brilliantly lit by the full moon. It seemed she was romantically inclined for she sat down by the window and fell into a dream of musing. Never (she used to recall, with streaming tears), never had she felt more

at peace with all men or thought more kindly of the world. As she sat, she became aware of an aged gentleman advancing along the lane; walking towards him was another very small gentleman. When they were near each other, the older man bowed and greeted the other with a very nice manner of politeness. He seemed to be inquiring his way. The moon shone on his face as he spoke and the girl was pleased to watch it; it was a noble, high-born face, and seemed to be filled with an innocent and old-world kindness. Presently her eye wandered to the other and she was surprised to recognise him as a certain Mr Hyde, who had once visited her master and for whom she had conceived a dislike. He was carrying a heavy cane; he seemed to listen to the old gentleman with ill-contained impatience. And then all of a sudden he broke out in a great flame of anger, stamping with his foot, brandishing the cane and behaving generally like a madman. The old gentleman took a step back, with the air of someone very much

surprised and a trifle hurt; and at that Mr Hyde broke out of all bounds and clubbed him to the earth. The next moment, with ape-like fury, he was trampling his victim underfoot and raining down blows, under which the unfortunate gentleman's bones were audibly shattered and the body jumped upon the roadway. At this point, the maid had fainted.

It was two o'clock when she called the police. The murderer was gone but in the middle of the road lay his victim, incredibly mangled. The stick with which he had been killed, although it was of some rare and very tough and heavy wood, had broken in the middle under the stress of this cruelty; one splintered half had rolled into the gutter — the other must have been carried away by the murderer. A purse and a gold watch were found upon the victim but no cards or papers except a sealed and stamped envelope, which he had probably intended to post, and which was addressed to Mr Utterson.

This was brought to the lawyer the next morning before he was out of bed, and as soon as he had heard the circumstances, he said solemnly, "I shall say nothing till I have seen the body. This may be very serious. Have the kindness to wait while I dress."

And with the same grave face he hurried through his breakfast and drove to the police station, where the body was kept. As soon as he saw it, he nodded.

"Yes," said he, "I recognise him. I'm sorry to say that this is Sir Danvers Carew."

"Good God, sir!" exclaimed the officer. "Is it possible?"

And the next moment his eyes lighted up.

"This will make a great deal of noise," he said. "And perhaps you can help us to the man."

And he then briefly narrated what the maid had seen, and showed the broken stick.

Mr Utterson had already cringed at the name of Hyde; on seeing the stick, even in its broken and battered state, he recognised it as

the one that he had presented many years ago to Henry Jekyll.

"The maid describes Mr Hyde as being particularly small and wicked-looking," added the officer.

Mr Utterson reflected, and then said, "I think I can take you to his house."

By this time it was about nine in the morning, it was quite foggy. A great chocolate-coloured pall hung over the sky, and as the carriage crawled from street to street, Mr Utterson admired a marvellous number of degrees and hues of twilight. Here it would be dark like the back-end of evening; and there would be a glow of a rich, lurid brown, like the light of some strange conflagration; and here, for a moment, the fog would be quite broken up, and a haggard shaft of daylight would glance in between the swirling wreaths. The dismal quarter of Soho seen in this light with its muddy ways, its dirty passengers and its lamps shining mournfully through,

seemed, in the lawyer's eyes, and to his gloomy mind, like some city in a nightmare.

As the carriage drew up before the address indicated, the fog lifted a little and showed him a dingy street, a gin palace, a low French eating-house, many ragged children huddled in the doorways and many women of different nationalities passing out, key in hand, to have a morning glass. The next moment the fog settled down again upon the scene, as brown as umber, and cut him off from his blackguardly surroundings. This was the home of Henry Jekyll's favourite; of a man who was heir to a quarter of a million sterling.

An ivory-faced old woman opened the door. She had an evil face smoothed by hypocrisy but her manners were excellent. Yes, she said, this was Mr Hyde's residence, but he was not at home; he had come home very late last night and had left again in less than an hour. There was nothing strange in that, she said. His habits were very irregular, and he was often absent; for instance,

it was nearly two months since she had seen him till yesterday.

"Very well, then, we wish to see his rooms," said the lawyer and when the woman began to protest, he added,"This person happens to be Inspector Newcomen of Scotland Yard."

A flash of evil joy appeared upon the woman's face.

"Ah!" said she, "he is in trouble! What has he done?"

Mr Utterson and the inspector exchanged glances. "He doesn't seem to be a very popular character," observed the latter. "And now, my good woman, just let us have a look around."

The house was empty except for the old woman. Mr Hyde had only used a couple of rooms but these were furnished with luxury and good taste. A closet was filled with wine; the plate was of silver, the elegant household napkin; a good picture hung upon the walls, a gift (as Mr Utterson supposed) from Jekyll, who was a connoisseur of art; the carpets were agreeable too. At the moment, however, the rooms looked like they had been recently and hurriedly ransacked; clothes lay about the floor with their pockets inside out; drawers stood open and on the hearth there lay a pile of grey ashes, as if many papers had been burned. From these embers the inspector retrieved the remains of a green cheque book. The other half of the stick, which was used to murder Sir Danvers Carew, was found behind the door and as this clinched his suspicions, the officer was delighted. A visit to the bank, where several thousand pounds were found to be lying to the murderer's credit, completed his gratification.

"You may depend upon it, sir," he told Mr Utterson, "I have him in my hand. He must have lost his head or he never would have left the stick or, above all, burned the cheque book. Why, we just have to wait for him at the bank."

This however, was not so easy to accomplish, for very few people seemed to know Mr Hyde. Even the old servant had only seen him twice;

his family could not be traced; he had never been photographed; the few who could describe him differed widely in their descriptions, as common observers would. They agreed only on one point and that was the haunting sense of deformity with which the fugitive had impressed his beholders.

Chapter Five

The Suspicious Letter

By the time Mr Utterson reached Dr Jekyll's house, it was late in the afternoon. He was immediately admitted by Poole, and escorted past the kitchen quarters and across a yard which had once been a garden, to the building which was indifferently known as the laboratory or the dissecting-room (the doctor had bought the house from the heirs of a celebrated surgeon). It was the first time that the lawyer had been received in that part of his friend's quarters. He eyed the dingy, windowless structure with curiosity and gazed round with a distasteful sense of strangeness as he crossed the theatre, once crowded with eager students

and now lying gaunt and silent, the tables laden with chemical apparatus, the floor strewn with crates and littered with packing straw with the light falling dimly through the foggy cupola. At the further end, a flight of stairs mounted to a door covered with red baize and through this Mr Utterson was at last received into the doctor's room. It was a large room, fitted round with glass presses, furnished, among other things, with a full-length looking glass and a business table, and looking out upon the court by three dusty windows barred with iron. A fire burned in the fireplace; a lamp burnt on the chimney shelf for the fog crept in thickly even inside the houses and there, drawn close up to the fire sat Dr Jekyll, looking deadly sick. He did not rise to meet his visitor, but held out a cold hand and bade him welcome in a changed voice.

"And now," said Mr Utterson, as soon as Poole had left them, "you have heard the news?"

The doctor shuddered. "I heard them crying it out in the square," he replied.

"I hope you haven't been mad enough to hide this fellow?" asked the lawyer.

"Utterson, I swear to God," cried the doctor, "I swear to God I will never set eyes on him again. Upon my honour, I'm done with him. It's all over. And indeed, he does not want my help; you do not know him as I do; he is safe, he is quite safe; mark my words, he will never more be heard of."

The lawyer listened gloomily; he did not like his friend's feverish manner.

"For your sake, I hope you're right," said he. "If it comes to a trial, your name might appear."

"I'm quite sure," replied Dr Jekyll, "I have grounds for being certain that I cannot share with anyone. But there is one thing on which you may advise me. I have—I have received a letter, and I'm at a loss whether I should show it to the police. I should like to leave it in your hands, Utterson; you would judge wisely, I'm sure; I trust you fully."

"Are you afraid that it might lead to his detection?" asked the lawyer.

"You who have so many things repair for a thousand generosities need not be alarmed for my safety.

Edward Hyde

"No," said the other. "I was thinking more of my own character, which this hateful business has rather exposed."

Mr Utterson pondered for a while; his friend's selfishness surprised, yet relieved him.

"Well," said he, at last, "let me see the letter."

The letter was written in an odd, upright hand and signed "Edward Hyde"; it briefly stated that the writer's benefactor, Dr Jekyll, whom he had long so unworthily repaid for a thousand generosities, need not be alarmed for his safety as he had his own sure means of escape. The lawyer thought that the letter showed the intimacy between Hyde and his friend in better colours than he had hoped for, and he blamed himself for some of his past suspicions.

"Do you have the envelope?" Mr Utterson asked.

"I burned it without thinking," replied Dr Jekyll. "But it bore no postmark. The note was handed in."

"Shall I keep this and sleep upon it?" asked Mr Utterson.

"I wish you to judge for me entirely," was the reply. "I have lost confidence in myself."

"Well, I shall consider," said the lawyer. "One word more: was it Hyde who dictated the terms in your will about that disappearance?"

The doctor seemed to be seized with a qualm of faintness: he shut his mouth tight and nodded.

"I knew it," said Mr Utterson. "He meant to murder you. You've had a fine escape."

"I've had something far more important," said the doctor solemnly. "I've had a lesson—Oh! God, Utterson, what a lesson I've had!"

And he covered his face with his hands.

On his way out, the lawyer stopped and had a word with Poole.

"By the by," said he, "there was a letter handed in today: what was the messenger like?"

Poole was positive nothing had come by post except circulars. Mr Utterson's fears were renewed. Plainly the letter had come by the

laboratory door; it might have been written in the room, and if that was the case, it must be differently judged, and handled with more caution.

The newsboys, as he went, were crying themselves hoarse along the footways: "Special edition. Shocking murder of an M. P."

That was the funeral oration of one friend and client, and he could not help feeling apprehensive lest the good name of another should be sucked down in the eddy of the scandal. It was a ticklish decision that he had to make, and though a self-reliant man by habit, he began to long for advice.

In the evening, he sat on one side of his own hearth with Mr Guest, his head clerk, on the other, and midway between them was a bottle of old wine that had long lived unsunned in the foundations of his house. The fog still slept on the wing above the drowned city where the lamps glimmered like gemstones, and the sounds of the town's life still rolled in with a sound like that of a mighty wind. But the room was gay with firelight, and the wine was mellow. Finally Mr Utterson found himself considering. There was no man

from whom he kept fewer secrets than Guest, and he was not always sure that he kept as many as he meant to. Guest was familiar with Dr Jekyll and his household, he must also have heard of Mr Hyde's familiarity about the house; he might draw conclusions: and above all Guest, being a great student and critic of handwriting, might shed fresh light on the case. The clerk, besides, was a man of counsel; any remark he might drop after reading the strange document might shape the future course chosen by the lawyer.

"This is a sad business about Sir Danvers," he said.

"Yes, sir, it has excited a great deal of public interest," returned Guest. "The man, of course, was mad."

"Guest, I have a document here in his handwriting," said the lawyer. "I would like your views upon it. Let this be in confidence between ourselves, for it is an ugly business."

Guest's eyes brightened, and he studied the document with passion.

"No, sir," he said, "not mad but it is an odd hand."

Just then the servant entered with a note.

"Is that from Dr Jekyll, sir?" inquired the clerk. "I thought I knew the writing. Anything private, Mr Utterson?"

"Only an invitation to dinner. Why? Do you want to see it?"

"Yes, for a moment. Thank you, sir," and the clerk laid the two sheets of paper alongside and diligently compared them.

"It's a very interesting autograph," he said at last, returning both.

"Why did you compare them, Guest?" inquired Mr Utterson suddenly.

"Well, sir," returned the clerk, "there's rather a striking resemblance; the two hands are in many points identical: only differently sloped."

"I wouldn't mention this to anyone," said Mr Utterson, somewhat disturbed.

"No, sir," said the clerk. "I understand."

POLICE NOTICE

£5,000 REWARD

Wanted for the murder of Sir Danvers Carew

Edward Hyde

Chapter Six

The Death of Dr Lanyon

Time passed. Thousands of pounds were offered in reward for the murderer, for the death of Sir Danvers was resented as a public injury. But Mr Hyde had disappeared as though he had never existed. Much of his disreputable past was unearthed: tales of the man's cruelty, callous and violent; of his vile life, and of his strange associates, but of his present whereabouts, not a whisper. From the time he had left the house in Soho on the morning of the murder, he was simply blotted out and gradually, with time, Mr Utterson began to recover from his alarm and grew more at peace with himself. The death of Sir Danvers

was, he thought, more than compensated for by the disappearance of Mr Hyde.

With the latter's evil influence gone, a new life began for Dr Jekyll. He came out of his seclusion, renewed relations with his friends, became once more their familiar guest and entertainer and while he had always been known for charities, he was now no less distinguished for religion. He was busy, he was seen a lot out in the open air; his face seemed to open and brighten, as if with an inward consciousness of service and for more than two months, the doctor was at peace.

On the 8th of January Mr Utterson had dined at Dr Jekyll's with a small party; Dr Lanyon had been there; it had been like the old days when the trio were inseparable friends. But on the 12th and again on the 14th, the lawyer found Dr Jekyll's door shut against him.

"The doctor was confined to the house," Poole said, "and saw no one."

On the 15th, he was again refused and in recent times accustomed to seeing his friend almost

daily, he found this return of solitude weighing upon his spirits. The fifth night he invited Guest to dine with him and on the sixth he paid Dr Lanyon a visit.

When he came face-to-face with the doctor, he was shocked at Dr Lanyon's changed appearance. He seemed to have his death warrant written upon his face. The rosy man had grown pale; his flesh had fallen away; he was visibly balder and older yet it was not so much the swift physical decay that arrested the lawyer's notice, as the appearance of some deep-seated terror of the mind. *He is a doctor*, thought Mr Utterson, *and he must know that his days are numbered, and the knowledge is more than he can bear.*

"I've had a shock," said Dr Lanyon, "and I shall never recover. It is a question of weeks. Well, life has been pleasant; I liked it; yes, sir, I used to like it. But I sometimes think if we knew all, we should be more than glad to get away."

"Jekyll is ill too," observed Mr Utterson. "Have you seen him?"

Dr Lanyon's face changed and he held up a trembling hand.

"I wish to see or hear no more of Dr Jekyll," he said in a loud, unsteady voice. "I am quite done with that person and I beg you not to mention his name."

"Can't I do anything?" inquired Mr Utterson after a considerable pause. "We three are very old friends, Lanyon; we shall not live to make others."

"Nothing can be done," said Lanyon, "ask the man himself."

"He won't see me," said the lawyer.

"I'm not surprised," was the reply. "Someday, Utterson, after I'm dead, you may perhaps learn the truth—I cannot tell you now. And in the meantime, if you can sit and talk with me of other things, for God's sake, stay and do so, but if you cannot keep clear of this topic then in God's name, go; I cannot bear it."

As soon as he got home, Mr Utterson wrote to Dr Jekyll, complaining of being denied entry to his house, and asking the cause of his unhappy

break with Dr Lanyon. The next day he received a long answer, often very pathetically worded, and sometimes darkly mysterious in drift. The quarrel with Dr Lanyon was incurable.

"I do not blame our old friend," Dr Jekyll wrote, "but I agree that we must never meet. I mean from henceforth to lead a life of extreme seclusion; you must not be surprised, nor must you doubt my friendship if my door is often shut even to you. You must allow me to go my own dark way. I have brought on myself a punishment and a danger that I cannot name. If I am the greatest of sinners I am the greatest of sufferers also. You can do only one thing for me, Utterson, and that is to respect my silence without judgment."

Mr Utterson was amazed. The dark influence of Hyde had been withdrawn, the doctor had returned to his old way of life; a week ago, everything had seemed so cheerful and honourable, but now in a moment, friendship, peace of mind and the whole meaning of Dr

Jekyll's life seemed to be wrecked. There must be some deeper ground for Dr Lanyon's manner and words.

A week later Dr Lanyon took to his bed, and in less than a fortnight he was dead. His death affected the lawyer deeply. The night after the funeral, Mr Utterson locked himself into his business room, and by the light of a melancholy candle, drew out an envelope written by his deceased friend, and bearing his seal. It was emphatically superscribed with the words "PRIVATE: for the hands of G. J. Utterson ALONE and in case of his predecease, to be destroyed unread." The lawyer dreaded the contents, but his curiosity was aroused when he found a second sealed enclosure, marked by the words "not to be opened till the death or disappearance of Dr Henry Jekyll."

Mr Utterson could not trust his eyes. Yes, the word "disappearance" had reappeared here as in the mad will which he had long ago returned to Dr Jekyll. There the man Hyde might have dictated the terms, but here Dr Lanyon was using

the same phrase. What could it mean? Mr Utterson was tempted to open the envelope and dive at once to the bottom of these mysteries, but professional honour and faith to his dead friend were more binding obligations, and he refrained.

From that day onwards, Mr Utterson became diligent in his pursuit of Dr Jekyll. He thought of him kindly but his thoughts were filled with disquietude and fear. He called on the doctor repeatedly and he was perhaps equally relieved to be denied admittance. Perhaps, in his heart, he preferred to speak with Poole upon the doorstep, surrounded by the air and sounds of the open city rather than to be admitted into that house of voluntary bondage, and to sit and speak with its mysterious recluse.

Poole had no pleasant news to communicate. The doctor, it appeared, now more than ever confined himself to the laboratory, where he would sometimes even sleep; he had grown very silent; he did not read; it seemed as if he had something on his mind. Gradually Mr Utterson

became so used to hearing the same report, that in time he decreased the frequency of his visits.

It chanced on a Sunday, when Mr Utterson was on his usual walk with Mr Enfield, that they passed once again through the bystreet. When they reached the door, both stopped to gaze on it.

"Well," said Enfield, "that story's at an end at least. We shall never see more of Mr Hyde."

"I hope not," said Mr Utterson. "Did I ever tell you that I once saw him, and shared your feeling of repulsion?"

"It was inevitable," replied Mr Enfield. "And by the way, what an ass you must have thought me, not to know that this was a back way to Dr Jekyll's!"

"So you found that out, did you?" asked Mr Utterson. "Let's step into the court and take a look then."

The court was very cool and a little damp, and a little dark. Sitting close beside the windows, taking the air like some disconsolate prisoner, Mr Utterson saw Dr Jekyll. He looked very sad.

"Jekyll!" he cried. "I trust you're better?"

"I'm very low, Utterson," replied the doctor, drearily, "very low. It will not last long, thank God."

"You stay indoors too much," said the lawyer. "You should be out, whipping up the circulation like Mr Enfield and me. (This is my cousin—Mr. Enfield—Dr. Jekyll.) Why don't you get your hat and take a quick turn with us?"

"You're very good," sighed the other. "I should like to, very much but no, no, no, it's quite impossible; I dare not. But indeed, Utterson, I'm very glad to see you; this is really a great pleasure. I would ask you and Mr Enfield up, but the place is really not fit."

"Why then," said the lawyer, good-naturedly, "the best thing we can do is to stay down here and speak with you from where we are."

"That is just what I was about to propose," said the doctor with a smile. But the words were hardly uttered before the smile was struck out of his face and succeeded by an expression of

such abject terror and despair that it froze the very blood of the two gentlemen below. They glimpsed it only for a moment for the window was instantly thrust down but that glimpse had been sufficient, and they turned and left the court without a word.

They walked down the bystreet in silence, and it was not until they had come into a neighbouring thoroughfare, where even on a Sunday there were still some stirrings of life, that Mr Utterson at last turned and looked at his companion. They were both pale, and there was horror in his companion's eyes.

"God forgive us, God forgive us," said Mr Utterson.

But Mr Enfield only nodded his head very seriously. They walked on again in silence.

Chapter Seven

Unexpected and Urgent Summons

Mr Utterson was sitting by his fireside one evening after dinner when he was surprised to receive a visit from Poole.

"Bless me, Poole, what brings you here?" he asked, and then taking a second look at him, he added, "Is the doctor ill?"

"Mr Utterson," replied Poole, "there is something wrong."

"Take a seat, and here is a glass of wine for you," said the lawyer. "Now, take your time, and tell me plainly what has happened."

"You know the doctor's ways, sir," replied Poole, "and how he shuts himself up. Well, he's shut himself up again in his room, and I don't like it, sir — Mr Utterson, sir, I'm afraid."

"Now, my good man," said the lawyer, "be clear. What are you afraid of?"

"I've been afraid for about a week," said Poole, doggedly disregarding the question, "and I can bear it no more."

The man's appearance amply bore out his words; he looked scared, and not once did he meet the lawyer's eyes. His held his glass of wine untasted on his knee, and continued to stare at the floor.

"I can bear it no more," he repeated.

"Come, Poole" said the lawyer, "I see there is something seriously wrong. Try to tell me what it is."

"I think there's been foul play," said Poole, hoarsely.

"Foul play!" cried the lawyer, frightened. "What foul play?"

"I daren't say, sir," was the answer; "will you come along with me and see for yourself?"

Mr Utterson's only answer was to rise and get his hat and coat, and to follow Poole to his old friend's quarters.

It was a wild, cold night of March, with a pale moon lying on her back as though the wind had tilted her, and a translucent, flying mass of clouds was floating by. The wind made talking difficult. It seemed to have swept the streets unusually empty of passengers for Mr Utterson thought he had never seen that part of London so deserted. And never in his life had he so wanted to see and touch his fellow men; his mind was weighed down by a crushing anticipation of calamity.

The square, when they got there, was all full of wind and dust, and the thin trees in the garden were lashing themselves along the railing. In spite of the biting weather, Poole took off his hat and mopped his brow with a red pocket-handkerchief. His face was white and his voice harsh and broken.

"Well, sir," he said, "here we are, and God grant that there is nothing wrong."

The servant knocked on the door in a very guarded manner. The door was opened with the chain restraining it, and a voice asked cautiously from within, "Is that you, Poole?"

"Yes," said Poole. "Open the door."

The hall was brightly lighted; the fire was built high; all the servants stood huddled together about the hearth like a flock of sheep. At the sight of Mr Utterson, the housemaid broke into hysterical whimpering, and the cook cried out, "Bless God! It's Mr Utterson!"

"They're all afraid," said Poole.

Silence followed, broken only by the loud wails of the maid.

"Hold your tongue!" Poole snapped, with a ferocity that testified to his own jangled nerves.

Chapter Eight

The Creature in the Room

Poole begged Mr Utterson to follow him, and led the way to the back garden.

"Now, sir," said he, "come as gently as you can. I want you to hear, and I don't want you to be heard. And if by any chance he asks you in, don't go."

Mr Utterson's nerves gave a jerk that nearly threw him off-balance but he summoned up courage and followed the butler into the laboratory building and through the surgical theatre, with its crates and bottles, to the foot of the stair. Here Poole signalled to him to stand on one side and listen, while he himself, setting

down the candle and obviously making a great call on his resolution, mounted the steps and knocked uncertainly on the room's door.

"Mr Utterson, sir, is asking to see you," he called, and once more signed to the lawyer to listen carefully.

A voice answered from within, "Tell him I cannot see any one."

"Thank you, sir," said Poole, with a note of something like triumph in his voice and taking up his candle, he led Mr Utterson back across the yard and into the great kitchen.

"Sir," he said, looking Mr Utterson in the eyes, "was that my master's voice?"

"It seems much changed," replied the lawyer, very pale, answering look for look.

"Changed? Well, yes, I think so," said the butler. "I've been twenty years in his service, and won't be deceived about his voice. No, sir, somebody's done away with the master—eight days ago—when we heard him cry out upon the name of God. Who's in there instead of him, and

why it stays there, is a thing that only Heaven knows, Mr Utterson!"

"This is a very strange tale, Poole; this is rather a wild tale, my man," said Mr Utterson, biting his finger. "Suppose it were as you suppose, supposing Dr Jekyll has been — well, murdered, what could induce the murderer to stay? That isn't reasonable."

"Well, Mr Utterson, you're a hard man to satisfy, but I'll do it yet," said Poole. "The whole of last week, whatever it is that lives in that room, has been crying out night and day for some sort of medicine. It was sometimes the master's way to write his orders on a sheet of paper and throw it on the stairs. This week we've had nothing but papers and a closed door, even the meals left there have been smuggled in only when nobody was looking. Well, sir, every day, and even twice or thrice in the same day, there have been orders and complaints, and I have been sent flying to all the wholesale chemists in town. Every time I brought the stuff back, there would be another paper

telling me to return it because it was impure, and another order to a different firm. This drug is wanted badly, sir, whatever for."

"Have you any of these papers?" asked Mr Utterson.

Poole felt in his pocket and handed out a crumpled note, which the lawyer, bending nearer to the candle, carefully examined. Its contents ran thus: "Dr Jekyll presents his compliments to Messrs Maw. He tells them that their last sample was impure and quite useless to him. In the year 18 —, Dr J. purchased a large quantity of the same from Messrs M. He now begs them to search most carefully, and should any of the same quality be left, to forward it to him at once. Expense is no consideration. This is vitally important to Dr J." So far the letter had run composedly enough, but here with a sudden splutter of the pen, the writer's emotion had broken loose. "For God's sake," he had added, "find me some of the old."

"This is a strange note," said Mr Utterson and then sharply added, "Did you open it yourself?"

"The man at Maw's was angry, sir, and he threw it back to me," said Poole.

"This is unquestionably the doctor's handwriting, do you know?" asked the lawyer.

"I thought it looked like it," said the servant, "but handwriting doesn't matter! I've seen him!"

"Seen him?" repeated Mr Utterson. "Well?"

"That's it!" said Poole. "It was this way. I came suddenly into the surgical theatre from the garden. It seems he had slipped out to look for this drug; his room's door was open, and there he was at the far end of the room, digging among the crates. He looked up when I came in, gave a cry and ran away. I saw him only for a moment, but the hair stood upon my head. Sir, if that was my master, why had he a mask upon his face? If it was my master, why did he cry out like a rat and run from me? I have served him long enough."

"This is all very strange," said Mr Utterson, "but I think I begin to see the light. Your master, Poole, must be seized with one of those illnesses that both torture and deform the sufferer; the alteration of his voice, the mask and his

avoidance of his friends may all be attributed to this; hence, his eagerness to find this drug, by which the poor soul hopes of recovery! That is my explanation. It is sad enough, Poole, and shocking as well but it is natural, hangs well together, and delivers us from serious alarms."

"Sir," said the butler, turning pale, "that thing was not my master, and that's the truth. My master" here he looked around him and began to whisper — "is a tall man of fine build, and this was more of a dwarf."

Mr Utterson attempted to protest.

"O, sir," cried Poole, "do you think I don't know my master after twenty years? Do you think I don't know to what height his head reaches in the room's door? No, sir, that thing in the mask was not Dr Jekyll — God knows what it was, but it was not Dr Jekyll, and in my heart I believe that he has been murdered."

"Poole," replied the lawyer, "if you say that, it will become my duty to make certain, and to break in that door."

"Ah! Mr Utterson, that's more like it!" cried the butler.

"And now comes the second question," resumed Mr Utterson, "Who is going to do it?"

"Why, you and me," was the brave reply.

"That's very well said," said the lawyer "and whatever happens, I shall ensure that you are not blamed."

"There is an axe in the theatre," said Poole, "and you might take the kitchen poker for yourself."

The lawyer took the crude but weighty instrument into his hand, and balanced it.

"This masked figure that you saw, did you recognise it?" he asked.

"Well, sir, the creature was doubled up and moved really fast. But if you mean, was it Mr Hyde? Why, yes, I think it was! It was as big as he, and it had the same quick, light movement. I hope you haven't forgotten, sir, that at the time of the murder he had still the key of the laboratory door with him. But that's not all. If ever you have met this Mr Hyde, then you must know that there was something queer about that gentleman; he evoked a kind of cold feeling in your very marrow."

"I also felt something like that," agreed Mr Utterson.

"Well, sir, when that masked thing jumped like a monkey and whipped into the room, that same feeling went down my spine like ice," said Poole. "Oh, I know it's not evidence, Mr Utterson. I'm book-learned enough for that but I give you my word on the Bible that it was Mr Hyde!"

"I see," said the lawyer. "My fears point in the same direction. I believe you; I believe poor Henry is killed and I believe his murderer is still lurking in the victim's room. Call Bradshaw."

The footman arrived, very white and nervous.

"Pull yourself together, Bradshaw," said the lawyer. "Poole and I are going to force our way into the room. If all is well, my shoulders are broad enough to bear the blame. Meanwhile, if anything is really amiss, or if the culprit tries to escape by the back, you and the boy must arm yourselves with a pair of good sticks and intercept them. You have ten minutes to get to your stations."

Chapter Nine

The Disappearance of a Friend

As Bradshaw left, the lawyer looked at his watch. "And now, Poole, let us get to ours," he said, and then led the way into the yard. The moon was covered with clouds, and it was now quite dark. The wind, breaking in puffs and draughts, tossed the flame of the candle to and fro. When they came into the shelter of the surgical theatre, they sat down silently to wait. London hummed solemnly all around, but nearer at hand, the stillness was only broken by the sounds of a footfall moving to and fro along the room's floor.

"So it will walk all day, sir," whispered Poole, "yes, and for most of the night. There's a bit of a

break only when a new sample comes from the chemist. Ah, it's an ill conscience that cannot rest! But listen again, a little closer Mr Utterson, and tell me, does that sound like the doctor's step?"

The steps fell lightly and oddly, with a certain swing, and slowly; it was different indeed from the heavy creaking tread of Dr Jekyll.

"Once," said Poole. "Once I heard it weeping!"

"Weeping?" asked the lawyer, conscious of a sudden chill.

"Weeping like a woman or a lost soul," said the butler. "With that sound in my heart, I could have wept too."

"Jekyll," cried Mr Utterson, in a loud voice, "I demand to see you."

There was no reply.

"I give you fair warning, our suspicions are aroused, and I must and shall see you," he resumed, "if not by fair means, then by brute force!"

"Utterson," said the voice, "for God's sake, have mercy!"

"Ah, that's not Jekyll's voice — it's Hyde's!" cried Mr Utterson."Down with the door, Poole!"

Poole swung the axe over his shoulder; the blow shook the building, and the red door leaped against the lock and hinges. A dismal screech of mere animal terror rang from the room. The wood was tough and the fittings of excellent workmanship, and it was not until the fifth blow that the lock burst and the wrecked door fell inwards on the carpet.

The intruders, shocked by their own riot and the succeeding stillness, stood back a little and peered in. There lay the room before their eyes in the quiet lamplight, a good fire glowing and chattering on the hearth, the kettle singing its thin strain, a drawer or two open, papers neatly organised on the business table, and nearer the fire, there were things laid out for tea: the quietest room that night in London, you would have said.

Right in the middle of the floor lay the contorted and still twitching body of a man. They drew near on tiptoe, turned it on its back

and beheld the face of Edward Hyde. He was dressed in clothes far too large for him, clothes of the doctor's size; the muscles of his face still moved with a semblance of life, but life was quite gone. There was a phial near him and a strong smell hung upon the air. Mr Utterson knew that he was looking on the body of a self-destroyer.

"We have come too late," he said sternly, "Hyde is gone wherever he is destined to go; it only remains for us to find the body of your master."

Most of the building was occupied by the surgical theatre, which filled almost the whole ground storey. The room formed an upper storey at one end and looked out upon the court. A corridor joined the theatre to the door on the bystreet, and with this the room communicated separately by a second flight of stairs. There were a few dark closets and a spacious cellar.

The lawyer and Poole thoroughly examined all these. Each closet was empty, and judging by the dust, had long stood unopened. Searching

the cellar useless as its entrance was found to be sealed up by a perfect mat of cobweb. There was no trace of Dr Jekyll anywhere, dead or alive.

"He may have fled," said Mr Utterson, turning to examine the door in the bystreet. It was locked. Lying nearby on the flags, they found the rusty key looking like it had not been used in a long time. On closer examination, it was found to be broken, as though a man had stamped on it.

The two men looked at each other, frightened. "This is beyond me, Poole," said the lawyer. "Let's go back to the room."

And with an occasional awestruck glance at the dead body, they proceeded to examine the room more thoroughly. At one table, there were traces of chemical work, various measured heaps of some white salt laid on glass saucers, as though for an experiment.

"That is the same drug that I was always bringing him," said Poole, and even as he spoke, the kettle with a startling noise boiled over.

This brought them to the fireside where the easy chair was drawn cosily up, and the things were laid out for tea; even the sugar was in the cup. A book, a pious work, for which Jekyll had often expressed a great esteem, lay open beside the tea-things. Mr Utterson was amazed to find it annotated, in the doctor's own hand, with startling blasphemies.

Next, the searchers came to the mounted looking glass, into whose depths they looked with an involuntary shiver. Their own pale and fearful faces looked back at them.

"This glass has seen some strange things, sir," whispered Poole.

What could Jekyll want with a mirror? wondered the lawyer in the same low tones.

Next they turned to the business-table. Among the neat array of papers on the desk, a large envelope was uppermost, and was addressed, in the doctor's hand, to Mr Utterson. The lawyer opened it and several enclosures fell to the floor.

The first was a will, drawn in the same eccentric terms as the earlier one, which he had returned six months before to Dr Jekyll, but, in place of the name of Edward Hyde, the lawyer was amazed to read the name of Gabriel John Utterson. He looked at Poole, and then back at the paper and finally at the dead man stretched upon the carpet.

"My head is reeling," he said. "He has possessed this document all these days; he had no reason to like me; he must have raged to see himself displaced yet he has not destroyed it!"

The next paper was a brief note in the doctor's hand and dated at the top.

"Oh Poole!" the lawyer cried, "he was alive and here today. He cannot have been murdered in so short a time, he must still be alive, he must have fled! But why? And how? And in that case, can we call this suicide? Oh, we must be careful. We may involve your master in danger."

"Why don't you read it, sir?" asked Poole.

"Because I'm afraid that I may cause it,"

replied the lawyer. But he took up the paper and read as follows:

My dear Utterson,

By the time this falls into your hands, I shall have disappeared, under what circumstances I cannot foresee, but my instinct tells me that the end is sure and must be early. Go then, and first read the narrative which Lanyon warned me he would place in your hands; and if you care to hear more, turn to the confession of

Your unworthy and unhappy friend,

HENRY JEKYLL.

"There was a third enclosure?" asked Mr Utterson.

"Here, sir," said Poole, and passed him a considerable-sized sealed packet. The lawyer put it in his pocket.

"I would say nothing of this to anybody," he said. "If your master has fled or is dead, we may at least save his reputation. It is now ten; I must go home and read these documents in quiet but I shall be back before midnight, and then we shall send for the police."

They went out, locking the door of the theatre behind them and Mr Utterson, once more leaving the servants gathered about the fire in the hall, trudged back to his office to read the two narratives in which the mystery was to be explained.

Chapter Ten

Dr Lanyon's Narrative

Four days ago, on the ninth of January, I received by the evening delivery a registered envelope, addressed in the hand of my colleague and old school companion, Henry Jekyll. This took me by surprise for we were by no means in the habit of correspondence. I had seen the man and dined with him the night before, and I couldn't imagine what he would want to communicate with me in writing. The contents of the letter increased my wonder; this is what it said:

10 December, 18 —

Dear Lanyon, You are one of my oldest friends; and although we may have differed

at times on scientific questions, I cannot remember, at least on my side, any break in our affection. If you had ever said to me, Jekyll, my life, my honour, my reason, depend upon you, I would have sacrificed my left hand to help you. Lanyon, my life, my honour and my reason, are now all at your mercy if you fail me tonight, I am lost. I'm not asking you for something dishonourable. But judge for yourself.

I want you to postpone all other engagements for tonight and to drive straight to my house. Poole, my butler, has his orders; you will find him awaiting your arrival with a locksmith. The door of my room is then to be forced: and you are to go in alone; to open the glazed press (letter E) on the left hand, breaking the lock if necessary and to draw out the fourth drawer from the top (or the third from the bottom). The right drawer may also be recognised by its contents: some powders, a phial and a paper book. I beg of you to carry back this drawer with you to Cavendish Square exactly as it stands.

That is the first part of the service: now for the second. The remaining part of the job should preferably be done at an hour when your servants are in bed. At midnight then I request you to be alone in your consulting room, and to admit with your own hand into the house a man who will present himself in my name and to place the drawer in his hands. With this, you will have played your part and earned my gratitude completely. Five minutes afterwards if you insist upon an explanation, you will get it, and in the process understand how crucial these things are to me; that by neglecting any one of them, fantastic as they must appear, you might cause my death or the shipwreck of my reason.

I am confident that you will not trifle with this appeal, yet my heart sinks and my hand trembles at the bare thought of this possibility. Think of me at this hour under a blackness of distress that cannot be exaggerated, and know that if you will only punctually do what I ask

of you, my troubles will roll away like a story that is told. Save me, dear Lanyon.

Your friend,

H. J.'

After reading this letter, I felt certain that my colleague was insane, but I also felt bound to do as he requested. An appeal worded thus could not be dismissed lightly. So I got into a hansom and drove straight to Jekyll's house. The butler was waiting; he had received by the same post a registered letter of instruction, and had a locksmith and a carpenter ready. We moved in a body to the old surgical theatre from which (as you are doubtless aware) Jekyll's private room can be entered most conveniently. The door was very strong, the lock excellent. The carpenter said that it was a difficult job, and the door would be badly damaged if that kind of force was used; the locksmith was near despair. But they were handy fellows, and after two hours of labour, the door stood open. The press marked E was

unlocked; I took out the drawer, had it filled up with straw and tied in a sheet, and returned with it to Cavendish Square.

Here I proceeded to examine its contents. The powders were neatly packed, but not with the precision of the chemist; Jekyll must have packed them himself. It was a simple crystalline salt of a white colour. The phial was about half-full of a blood red liquor, highly pungent-smelling, and seemed to me to contain phosphorus and some volatile ether. I could make no guess about the other ingredients. The book contained little but a series of dates, covering a period of many years. The entries had stopped nearly a year ago and quite abruptly. Here and there a brief remark was appended to a date, usually no more than a single word: "double" occurring perhaps six times in a total of several hundred entries; and once very early in the list and followed by several exclamation marks, the words "total failure!!!" All this whetted my curiosity but revealed little. How could a salt, a phial and a record of failed

experiments affect either the honour, the sanity or the life of my flighty colleague? If his messenger could come to my house, why couldn't he go his own? And why was this gentleman to be received by me in secret? The more I reflected, the more convinced I grew that I was dealing with a case of cerebral disease, and after dismissing my servants, I loaded an old revolver for self-defence.

Twelve o'clock had scarcely rung out over London when I heard a low, careful knock on the door. I found a small man crouching against the pillars of the portico.

"Has Dr Jekyll sent you?" I asked.

He nodded with a strained gesture and when I asked him to enter, he threw a furtive backward glance into the darkness of the square and then obeyed. As I followed him into the bright light of the consulting room, I kept my hand ready on my weapon. Here I could see him clearly. He was small but I was struck most with the shocking expression of his face, with the impression he gave of great muscular activity and great

apparent illness, and—last but not least—with the odd disturbance I felt in his vicinity. It felt like the onset of rigour and was accompanied by a marked sinking of the pulse. At the time, I dismissed it as some idiosyncratic, personal distaste, but since then I have had reason to believe that the cause of this lay much deeper.

This person who had thus struck me with a feeling of disgusted curiosity was dressed in a fashion that would have made an ordinary person laughable; his clothes though they were of rich and sober fabric were big for him—the trousers hanging on his legs and rolled up to keep them from the ground, the waist of the coat below his haunches, the collar sprawling widely on his shoulders. But this ludicrous sense of dressing was far from moving me to laughter. Rather, it seemed to reinforce that which was elusively abnormal and badly conceived in the very essence of the creature— something that seized, surprised and revolted me.

My visitor seemed to be on fire with excitement and tension.

"Have you got it?" he cried. "Have you got it?" And he laid his hand upon my arm and shook me.

His touch made a cold shiver run down my spine, and I put his hand back.

"Come, sir," said I. "You forget that we are not even acquainted. Be seated, please."

And showing him a chair, I sat down myself in my customary seat, trying to enact my ordinary manner to a patient as much as I could, despite the lateness of the hour and the horror I felt for my visitor.

"I beg your pardon, Dr Lanyon," he replied civilly enough. "You are absolutely right; in my desperate impatience, I forgot politeness. I have been sent here by your colleague, Dr Henry Jekyll, on business of some considerable importance, and I understood ..." He paused and put his hand to his throat, and I could see, in spite of his collected manner, that he was wrestling against an onset of hysteria — "I understood, a drawer ..."

"There it is, sir," said I, pointing to the drawer, where it lay on the floor behind a table and still covered with the sheet.

He sprang towards it and then paused, and laid his hand upon his heart: I could hear his teeth grate convulsively; his face was so ghastly to see that I grew alarmed.

"Compose yourself," said I.

He turned a dreadful smile to me, and as if with the decision of despair, plucked away the sheet. At the sight of the contents, he uttered a loud sob of such immense relief that I sat petrified. And the next moment, in a voice that was already fairly well under control, he asked for a graduated glass. On my furnishing him with one, he thanked me, measured out a few minims of the red tincture and added one of the powders. As the crystals melted, the mixture, at first of a reddish hue, began to brighten in colour, to effervesce audibly and to throw off small fumes. Suddenly the bubbling stopped and the compound changed to a dark purple, which

faded again more slowly to a watery green. My visitor, who had watched these metamorphoses with a keen eye, smiled, set down the glass upon the table, and then turned and looked at me.

"And now," said he, "Will you be wise? Will you be guided? Will you allow me to take this glass and leave your house without further discussion? Or will you be commanded by the greed of curiosity? Think before you answer for it shall be as you decide. You will either be left none the richer nor wiser, or, if you so prefer, a new province of knowledge and new avenues to fame and power shall be laid open to you, here, in this room, this very instant; and your sight shall be blasted by a prodigy fit to stagger the disbelief of Satan."

"Sir," said I, trying to sound calmer than I felt, "you speak in riddles. But I've gone too far to pause before I see the end."

"All right," replied my visitor. "Lanyon, you remember your vows: what follows is under the seal of secrecy of our profession. And now, you who have so long bound yourself to the narrowest and most material views, you who have denied the potential of transcendental medicine — behold!"

He put the glass to his lips and drank at one gulp. A cry followed; he reeled, staggered, clutched at the table and held on, staring with protruding eyes and gasping. I noticed that there came a change — he seemed to swell — his face became suddenly black and the features seemed to melt and alter — and the next moment, I had sprung to my feet and leaped back against the wall, my arm raised to shield me from that prodigy, my mind submerged in terror.

"Oh God!" I screamed again and again for there before my eyes — pale and shaken, half-fainting and groping before him with his hands, like a man restored from death — there stood Jekyll!

What he told me next, I cannot bring myself to write. I saw what I saw, I heard what I heard and my soul sickened at it. My life is shaken to its roots; sleep has left me; I am haunted by the deadliest terror all day and night; I feel that my days are numbered, and that I must die; and yet I shall die incredulous. As for the moral depravity of that man, I cannot think of it without a start of horror. I will say but one thing, Utterson, and that will be more than enough. The creature who crept into my house that night was, on Jekyll's own confession, known by the name of Hyde and hunted for in every corner of the land as the murderer of Carew.

HASTIE LANYON

Chapter Eleven

Henry Jekyll's Full Statement of the Case

I was born in the year 18—to a large fortune, inclined by nature to work hard, fond of the respect of the wise and good among my fellow men, and thus with every guarantee of an honourable and distinguished future. The worst of my faults was a certain impatience and gaiety of disposition, which I found hard to reconcile with my arrogant desire to carry my head high, and wear a grave expression in public.

Hence it so happened that I concealed this pleasurable side of my life, and when I reached

maturer years of reflection, and began to take stock of my progress and position in the world, my life was already marked by a profound duplicity. Many would have publicly flaunted the kind of irregularities as I was guilty of but from the elevated viewpoint that I had fixed for myself, I hid them with an almost morbid sense of shame.

It was thus rather my own exacting nature than any particular degradation in myself that caused me to divide and separate the good and the bad aspects within me more absolutely than in the majority, where it lies in its natural state of duality. Although a double-dealer I was in no sense a hypocrite; both sides of me were in dead earnest. I was equally myself when I laid aside all restraint and plunged in shameful acts, and when I laboured all day at furthering knowledge or at relieving sorrow and suffering.

Moreover, it chanced that my scientific studies, which led wholly towards the mystic and the transcendental. With every day, and from both

sides of my intelligence, the moral and the intellectual, I thus drew steadily nearer to that truth, whose partial discovery has doomed me to such a dreadful shipwreck: that man is not truly one, but truly two. I say two because my own knowledge has not crossed that point. Others will outstrip me on the same lines; I hazard the guess that man will ultimately be known to be constituted by a community of multifarious, inappropriate and independent denizens. As for me, I learnt to see clearly that two thoroughly opposite natures contended in the field of my consciousness, and I was radically both.

From an early date, I had begun to dwell with pleasure, as in a beloved daydream, on the possibility of separating these two elements. If each, I reasoned, could be housed in separate identities, life would be relieved of tension. The unjust, delivered from higher aspirations and the remorse of his more upright twin might go his way, and the just could walk steadfastly and securely on his upward path, doing the good

things he wanted to do, and no longer vulnerable to disgrace in the hands of his degenerate twin. It was the curse of mankind that these polar twins, thus bound together in consciousness, should be continuously struggling. My question was — how could they be dissociated?

Through my experiments, I began to perceive more and more deeply the trembling immateriality, the mist-like transience of this seemingly solid body which we inhabit. I found that certain agents had the power to shake and to pluck back that garment of flesh, even as a wind might toss the curtains of a pavilion. For two good reasons, I will not enter deeply into this part. First, because I have learnt the hard way that when the attempt is made to separate a part of ourselves, it only returns with more awful pressure. Second, because, as my narrative will make too evident that my discoveries were incomplete. It is enough to say then that not only did I recognise my existing, natural body to be the mere projected aura of some of the powers that made up my

6

spirit, but also managed to compound a drug by which these powers could be dethroned from their supremacy, and a second form and appearance created, none the less natural to me because they were the expression, and bore the stamp of the lower elements of my soul.

I hesitated long before I put this theory to the test. I knew well that I risked death; any drug that so potently shook the very basis of identity, might by the least overdose utterly blot out that immaterial form, which I expected it to change. But the temptation of a discovery so singular and profound was stronger than the alarm I parallely felt. I had long since prepared my tincture; I now purchased, from a firm of wholesale chemists, a large quantity of a particular salt which was the last ingredient required. One late dreaded night, I compounded the elements, watched them boil and smoke together in the glass, and when the bubbling had subsided, resolutely drank off the potion.

The most racking pangs succeeded: a grinding in the bones, deadly nausea and a horror of the spirit that cannot be exceeded at the hour of birth or death. Then these agonies began swiftly to subside and I came to myself as if out of a great sickness. There was something strange in my sensations, something indescribably new and, from its very novelty, incredibly sweet. I felt younger, lighter, happier in body; within myself, I was conscious of a heady recklessness, a current of disordered sensual images, a dissolution of the bonds of obligation and an unknown freedom. I knew myself, at the first breath of this new life, to be more wicked, tenfold more wicked and the thought, in that moment, braced and delighted me like wine. I stretched out my hands, celebrating my new sensations, and in the act, I was suddenly aware that I had lost stature.

At that time there was no mirror in my room; that which stands here now was brought later on for the very purpose of witnessing these transformations. The time was close to dawn,

and the inmates of my house were locked in deep sleep. Flushed with hope and triumph, I decided to venture in my new shape to my bedroom. I crossed the yard; the stars looked down upon me, I thought with wonder — the first creature of that sort that they had seen during their unsleeping vigilance. I stole through the corridors, a stranger in my own house; in my room, I saw for the first time the appearance of Edward Hyde.

Here I must speak by theory alone; my explanation is not based on that which is known for certain, but that which I suppose to be most probable. The evil side of my nature, to which form I had now transformed, was less robust, less developed and younger than the good one which I had just deposed. The course of my life had been, after all, nine-tenths a life of effort, virtue and control; my degenerated self had been much less exercised and much less exhausted. And hence, I think, Edward Hyde was so much smaller, slighter and younger than Jekyll. Even as Jekyll bore the stamp of virtue, evil was written

plainly on the face of Hyde. Besides, evil had left on that body an imprint of deformity and decay. And yet when I looked upon that ugly figure in the glass, I felt no disgust, but rather of a leap of welcome. This, too, was I. It seemed natural and human, a more genuine reflection of myself than the conflicting and divided appearance I had so long had as Henry Jekyll. I have observed that when I was Edward Hyde, none could come near me without a visible doubts of the flesh. This was probably because all the human beings we meet are a compound of good and evil, and Edward Hyde, alone among men, was pure evil.

I lingered only a moment at the mirror: the second and conclusive experiment was yet to be attempted; it yet remained to be seen if I had lost my identity as Jekyll beyond redemption and must flee before daylight from a house that was no longer mine. Hurrying back to my room, I once more prepared and drank the cup, once more suffered the pangs of dissolution, and came to

myself once more with the character, the stature and the face of Jekyll.

The drug had no discriminating action; it was neither diabolical nor divine; it only shook the doors of the prison-house of my disposition, and that which was within ran out. At the time my honour slumbered, my evil aspect, alert and swift to seize the occasion, leaped forth, and the thing that was projected was Edward Hyde. Hence, although I had now two characters as well as two appearances, one was wholly evil, and the other was still the old Henry Jekyll, a bizarre compound of good and bad, of whose reformation and improvement I had already learnt to despair. Hyde was therefore not balanced by a completely good personality, and thus the movement was wholly towards the worse.

As my pleasures, even as Henry Jekyll, were (to say the least) undignified, and I was not only well-known and highly esteemed, but growing elderly as well, this aspect of my life was daily

becoming more unwelcome. It was here that my new power tempted me until I was bound in slavery. I had but to drink the cup, to shed at once the body of the noted professor, and to assume, like a thick cloak, that of Edward Hyde. I smiled at the notion; it struck me as humorous then; I made my preparations most carefully.

I took and furnished that house in Soho, to which Hyde was tracked by the police and engaged as housekeeper a creature whom I well knew to be silent and unscrupulous. Moreover, I announced to my servants that a Mr Hyde (whom I described) was to have full liberty and power about my — Jekyll's — house in the square. I next drew up that will to which you objected so much so that if anything befell me in the person of Dr Jekyll, I could enter on that of Edward Hyde without monetary loss. Thus fortified, as I supposed, on every side, I began to enjoy the strange immunities of my position.

Chapter Twelve

The Confessions of Hyde

In the past, men have hired bravos to transact their crimes, so as to shelter their reputation. I was the first who could live in the public eye with genial respectability, and in a moment, like a schoolboy, strip off these trappings and spring headlong into the sea of liberty. In my impenetrable disguise, the safety was complete. Let me but escape into my laboratory, give me but a second or two to mix and swallow the draught that is always standing ready. Whatever he had done, Edward Hyde would pass away like the stain of breath upon a mirror instead, quietly at home, trimming the midnight lamp in his study,

I would be an irreproachable man who could afford to laugh at suspicion—Henry Jekyll.

As I've already said, the pleasures which I enjoyed as Jekyll were undignified. In the hands of Edward Hyde, they soon began to turn monstrous. After returning from these excursions, I was often plunged into a kind of wonder at my depravity. This familiar being was inherently malign and villainous; his every act centred on himself; he drank pleasure with bestial interest; he was relentless like a man of stone. Henry Jekyll stood at times aghast before the acts of Edward Hyde but the situation was so extraordinary, the pinch of conscience relaxed gradually. It was Hyde, after all, and Hyde alone, who was guilty. Jekyll was no worse; he woke again to his good self seemingly weakened; he would even make haste, wherever possible, to undo the evil done by Hyde. And thus his conscience slept.

I have no intention of entering into the details of the wicked acts which I had committed (for even now I can scarcely grant that I did those).

I intend only to point out the warnings with which my punishment approached. On one occasion, I was forced to issue a cheque in the name of Henry Jekyll for the redressal of a wrong Hyde had committed towards a child, but this danger was easily removed from the future by opening an account at another bank in the name of Edward Hyde himself and when, by sloping my own hand backward, I had supplied my double with a signature, I thought I sat beyond the reach of fate.

Some two months before the murder of Sir Danvers, I had been out for one of my adventures, had returned at a late hour and woken the next day in bed with somewhat odd sensations. I looked around my familiar bedroom, but something kept insisting that I had not wakened where I seemed to be, but in the little room in Soho where I was accustomed to sleep in the body of Edward Hyde. Smiling to myself, I began to lazily reflect on my illusions, occasionally dropping back into a comfortable morning doze.

I was still thus engaged when, in one of my more wakeful moments, my eyes fell upon my hand. Now the hand of Henry Jekyll (as you have often remarked) was professional-looking, being large, firm, white and comely. But the hand which I now saw, clearly enough, in the yellow light of a mid-London morning, sitting in bed, was lean, corded, knuckly, of a dusky pallor and thickly shaded with a swart growth of hair. It was the hand of Edward Hyde.

I must have stared at it for nearly half a minute, sunk in the stupidity of wonder before terror was aroused in my breast as sudden and startling as the crash of alarms; bounding from my bed, I rushed to the mirror. At the sight that met, my eyes, my blood changed into something exquisitely thin and icy. Yes, I had gone to bed as Henry Jekyll, I had awakened as Edward Hyde. How was this to be explained? I asked myself, and then, with another bound of terror — how was it to be remedied? The morning was well advanced; the servants were up; all my drugs were in the

cabinet — a long journey down two pairs of stairs, through the back passage, across the open court and through the anatomical theatre. It might be possible to cover my face but how could I conceal the change in my stature? And then with an overpowering sweetness of relief, I remembered that the servants were already used to the coming and going of my second self. I had soon dressed, as well as I was able, in the clothes of Dr Jekyll, and passed through the house. Bradshaw stared at seeing Mr Hyde at such an hour and dressed so strangely in Jekyll's clothes, but ten minutes later, Dr Jekyll had returned to his own shape and was sitting down to make a pretence at eating heartily.

Small indeed was my appetite. I began to reflect more seriously than ever before on the issues and possibilities of my double existence. That part of me which I had the power of projecting, had lately been much exercised and nourished. It had recently seemed to me as though the body of Edward Hyde had grown in stature, as though (when I wore that form) a

more generous tide of blood flowed through my veins; I began to anticipate that, if this was much prolonged, the balance of my nature might be permanently overthrown, the power of voluntary change be forfeited, and make me permanently and irrevocably into Edward Hyde.

The power of the drug had not been always been the same. Once in the very early days, it had totally failed me; since then, on more than one occasion, I had been obliged to double, and once, with infinite risk of death, to treble the amount. Till date, it was these rare uncertainties that had cast the only shadow on my contentment. Now I was forced to take note of the fact that whereas, in the beginning, the difficulty had been to throw off the body of Jekyll, recently it had gradually but decidedly transferred itself to the other side. Everything therefore seemed to point to this: that I was slowly losing hold of my original and better self, and becoming slowly incorporated with my second and worse.

Between these two, I now felt I had to choose. My two natures had memory in common, but all other faculties were unequally shared between them. Jekyll was composite; he projected and shared in the pleasures and adventures of Hyde, sometimes with doubts, sometimes with a greedy gusto, but Hyde was indifferent to Jekyll, or just remembered him as the mountain bandit remembers the cave in which he conceals himself from pursuit. Jekyll had more than a father's interest; Hyde had more than a son's indifference. If I chose Jekyll I would have had to sacrifice those pleasures which I had long secretly indulged in and had recently begun to pamper. If I chose Hyde, I would have had to die to a thousand interests and aspirations and become despised and friendless. There was still another consideration in the bargain while Jekyll would suffer in the fires of abstinence, Hyde would be not even conscious of all that he had lost. Strange as my circumstances were, the terms of this debate are as old and commonplace as man; more

or less the same inducements and alarms cast the die for any tempted and trembling sinner; and it so happened with me, as it has happened with a vast a majority of my fellows, that I chose the better part but was found wanting in the strength to keep to it.

Yes, I preferred the discontented doctor, surrounded by friends and cherishing honest hopes. So I bade a resolute farewell to liberty, the comparative youth, the light step, leaping impulses and secret pleasures, that I had enjoyed in the disguise of Hyde. I made this choice perhaps with some unconscious reservation, for I neither gave up the house in Soho nor destroyed the clothes of Edward Hyde, which still lay ready in my cabinet. For two months I was true to my determination; for two months I led a life of unprecedented severity and enjoyed the approval of my conscience. But at last, time began to remove my alarm. Growing habituated to the praises of conscience, I began to be tortured again with throes and longings, as of Hyde struggling

to be free; at last, in an hour of moral weakness, I once again compounded and swallowed the transforming draught.

I do not suppose that when a drunkard reasons with himself upon his vice, he is once out of five hundred times affected by the dangers that he runs in his state of brutish, physical insensibility; neither had I made enough allowance for the complete moral insensibility and readiness to evil, which were the leading characteristics of Edward Hyde. My devil that had been long caged, he came out roaring. I was conscious, even when I took the draught, of a more unbridled, a more furious propensity to commit ill. It must have been this that caused me to attack my poor victim without provocation, as unreasonably as an impatient child breaking his toy. I had voluntarily stripped myself of all those balancing instincts by which even the worst of us continues to walk with some degree of steadiness among temptations; in my case, to be tempted, however slightly, was to fall.

And so that day, the spirit of Hell instantly awoke in me and raged. It was with glee that I mauled the unresisting body, delighting in every blow; it was not till weariness overcame me that I was suddenly, in the height of my delirium, struck through the heart by a cold thrill of terror.

A mist dispersed; I saw the ruin of my life and fled from the scene, at once glorying and trembling, my lust of evil gratified and stimulated, my love of life screwed to the topmost peg. I ran to the house in Soho and destroyed my papers then I set out through the lamplit streets, in the same divided ecstasy of mind, gloating on my crime, light-headedly devising others in the future.

Hyde had a song upon his lips as he compounded the draught, but the pangs of transformation had not yet left him, before Henry Jekyll, with streaming tears of gratitude and remorse, had fallen upon his knees and lifted his clasped hands to God. The veil of self-indulgence was there from head to foot, I saw my life as a whole: right from the days of childhood, when I had walked holding my father's hand, and through the self-denying toils of my professional life, to arrive again and again, with the same sense of unreality, at the horrors of the evening. I could have screamed aloud; with tears and prayers I tried to smother down the crowd of hideous images and sounds with which my memory swarmed.

When the acuteness of remorse gradually began to subside, it was succeeded by a sense of joy. The problem of my conduct was solved. Hyde was henceforth impossible; whether I wanted to or not, I was now confined to the better part of my existence; oh, how I rejoiced to think of it! With willing humility I embraced anew the restrictions of natural life! With sincere renunciation, I locked the door by which I had so often gone and come and ground the key under my heel.

The next day brought the news that the guilt of Hyde was known to the whole world, and that the victim was a man high in public estimation. I was glad; glad to have my better impulses thus reinforced and guarded by the terrors of the scaffold. Jekyll was now my city of refuge; let Hyde peep out an instant, and he would be captured and killed.

Chapter Thirteen

The Unhappy End of Dr Jekyll

I resolved to redeem the past through my future conduct and I can honestly say that my resolve did some good. You know yourself how earnestly in the last months of last year, I laboured to relieve suffering; you know that much was done for others, and that the days passed quietly, almost happily for myself. I can't truly say that I got weary of this beneficent and innocent life; I think instead that I daily enjoyed it more completely.

But cursed as I was with my singular duality, as the first edge of my regret wore off, the lower side of me, so long indulged, so recently chained down, began to growl for licence. Not that I dreamed of resuscitating Hyde; the bare idea

would drive me to frenzy. No, it was in my own person, as Dr Jekyll, that I once more indulged in those undignified pleasures. But there comes an end to all things; the last proverbial straw breaks the camel's back; this last brief indulgence of evil finally destroyed the balance of my soul. And yet I was not alarmed; the fall seemed natural like a return to the old days.

It was a fine, clear, January day, wet underfoot where the frost had melted, but cloudless overhead; the Regent's Park was full of winter chirrupings and sweet with spring odours. I sat in the sun on a bench; the animal within me licking the chops of memory; the spiritual side a little drowsy, when suddenly a qualm came over me, a horrid nausea and the most deadly shuddering. These passed away and left me faint, and then as the faintness subsided, I began to be aware of a change in the temper of my thoughts, a greater boldness, a contempt for danger, a dissolution of the bonds of obligation. I looked down; my clothes hung formlessly on my shrunken limbs; the muscles of my hand was corded and hairy.

I was once more Edward Hyde. A moment before I had been safe, worthy of everyone's respect, wealthy, beloved; now I was the common enemy of mankind, hunted, houseless, a known murderer destined for the gallows.

My reason wavered, but it did not fail me utterly. In my second character, I've often observed, my faculties seemed more sharpened and my spirits more elastic thus where Jekyll might perhaps have succumbed, Hyde rose to the importance of the moment. My drugs were in one of the presses of my room; how was I to reach them? That was the problem I set myself to solve. I had myself closed the laboratory door. If I tried to enter the house, my own servants would consign me to the gallows. I saw I must employ another hand, and thought of Lanyon. How was he to be reached? How was he to be persuaded? Supposing that I escaped capture in the streets, how was I to make my way into his presence? And how should I, an unknown and displeasing visitor, prevail on the famous

physician to rummage the study of his colleague, Dr Jekyll?

Then I remembered that I still retained one part of my original character: I could write my own hand.

Thereafter, I arranged my clothes as best I could, and summoning a passing hansom, drove to a hotel. At my appearance (which was indeed comical enough), the driver could not conceal his smile. I gnashed my teeth with a gust of devilish fury and the smile withered from his face — happily for him — yet more happily for myself, for in another instant I would have certainly dragged him from his perch.

At the inn, as I entered, I looked about me with such a black expression that the attendants trembled; they submissively took my orders, led me to a private room and brought me materials to write. Hyde in danger of his life was a creature new to me; shaken with inordinate anger, strung to the pitch of murder, lusting to inflict pain. Yet the creature was astute. He mastered his fury with a great effort of the will; composed his two

important letters to Lanyon and to Poole; and so that he might have actual evidence of their being posted, sent them out with directions that they should be registered.

He sat all day by the fire in the private room, gnawing his nails; there he dined, sitting alone with his fears, the waiter visibly shaking with fear before him, and then, with the darkness, he left in a carriage, and was driven to and fro about the streets of the city. When at last the driver had begun to grow suspicious, he got off the carriage and ventured out on foot, dressed in his misfitting clothes, into the midst of the nocturnal passengers, fear and anger raging within him. He walked fast, hunted by his fears, chattering to himself, skulking through the less-frequented thoroughfares, counting the minutes left till midnight. Once a woman spoke to him, offering, I think, a box of lights. He struck her in the face and she fled.

When I came to myself at Lanyon's, the horror of my old friend perhaps affected me somewhat. A change had come over me. It was no longer

the fear of the gallows, it was the horror of being Hyde that tormented me. I received Lanyon's condemnation partly in a dream; it was partly in a dream that I came home to my own house and got into bed.

I slept profoundly after the terrors of the day; not even the nightmares that wrung me could break my profound sleep. I awoke in the morning shaken, weakened, but refreshed. I still hated and feared the thought of the brute that slept within me, and of course I hadn't forgotten the appalling dangers of the day before, but I was once more at home, in my own house and close to my drugs; I was filled with gratitude.

I was stepping leisurely across the court after breakfast, drinking in the chill of the air with pleasure when I was seized again with those indescribable sensations that heralded the change. I was able to only just gain the shelter of my room before I was once again raging and freezing with the passions of Hyde. This time it took a double dose to recall me to myself, and alas! Six hours afterwards, as I sat looking sadly

in the fire, the pangs returned and the drug had to be re-administered. In short, from that day onwards, it seemed that I was able to hold on to the appearance of Jekyll only by a great effort, and only under the immediate stimulation of the drug. At any time, I could be taken with the unpleasant shudder; above all, if I slept, or even dozed for a moment in my chair, it was always as Hyde that I woke up.

Under the strain of this doom and by the sleeplessness to which I now condemned myself, I became, in my own person of Jekyll, a creature eaten up and emptied by fever, languidly weak both in body and mind, and solely occupied by one thought: the horror of my other self. But when I slept, or when the effects of the medicine wore off, I would find myself suddenly, almost without transition (for the pangs of transformation grew daily less marked), possessed of a fancy brimming with images of terror, a soul boiling with hatred and a body not strong enough to

contain the raging energies of life. The powers of Hyde seemed to have grown with the sickliness of Jekyll.

And certainly the hate that now divided them was equal on each side. With Jekyll, it was a thing of vital instinct. He had now seen the full deformity of that creature that shared his consciousness, and was co-heir with him to death: he now thought of Hyde as of something not only hellish but inorganic. And also, that insurgent horror was knit to him closer than a wife, closer than an eye; it lay caged in his flesh, where he heard it mutter and felt it struggle to be born; at every hour of weakness, and in sleep, prevailed against him and deposed him out of life.

The hatred of Hyde for Jekyll was of a different order. His terror of the gallows drove him continually to commit temporary suicide, and return to his subordinate station of a part instead of a person but he loathed the necessity, he loathed the despondency into which Jekyll

had now fallen and he resented the dislike with which Jekyll regarded him. Hence he would play ape-like tricks on Jekyll, scrawling blasphemies on the pages of his favourite books in the doctor's own hand, burning the letters and destroying the portrait of his father; indeed, had it not been for his fear of death, he would long ago have ruined himself in order to ruin me. But his love of life is wonderful; indeed, I who sickens at the mere thought of him will go further to say that when I recall his passionate attachment to life, and when I know how he fears my power to cut him off by suicide, I pity him.

It is useless, and the time is too short to prolong this description. Let it suffice to say that even to these torments, I was growing a certain callousness of soul and my punishment might have gone on for years, but for this last calamity.

My provision of the salt, which had never been re-purchased since the first experiment began to run low. I sent out for a fresh supply and mixed

the draught; the bubbling followed and with the first change of colour, not the second, I drank it.

Poole will tell you how I have had London ransacked; it was in vain and I am now convinced that my first supply was impure, and that it was that unknown impurity which lent efficacy to the draught.

About a week has passed, and I am now finishing this statement under the influence of the last of the old powders. This, then, is the last time, short of a miracle, that Henry Jekyll can think his own thoughts or see his own face in the mirror. I must not delay to bring my writing to an end for if the throes of change take me in the act of writing it, Hyde will at once tear it to pieces. But if some time is allowed to elapse after I have kept it aside, his wonderful self- absorption in the moment will probably save it once again from his ape-like spite.

And indeed the doom closing on us both has already changed and crushed him. Half an hour from now, when I shall again and forever assume that hated personality, I know how I shall sit shuddering and weeping in my chair or pace up and down this room with my ear tuned to every sound of menace.

Will Hyde die upon the scaffold? Or will he find the courage to release himself at the last moment? God knows; I am careless; this is my true hour of death, and what is to follow concerns someone other than myself. Here then, as I lay down my pen and proceed to seal up my confession, I bring the life of that unhappy Henry Jekyll to an end.

About the Author

▪ Robert Louis Stevenson

Robert Louis Stevenson was a Scottish novelist, poet, essayist and travel writer. He also has many original musical compositions to his credit.

Born in Edinburgh, Scotland, on 13 November 1850, he was the only child of Margaret and Thomas Stevenson, a pioneer in designing lighthouses. Stevenson's attendance at school was often interrupted because of his frequent illness, and he was taught for long stretches of time by private tutors.

Even before he learnt to read, Stevenson had begun dictating stories to his mother and nurse. He enrolled at Edinburgh University to study engineering, with the goal of following his father in the family business. Lighthouse design never appealed to Stevenson though and he began studying law instead. But being principally interested in travelling and writing, he broke away from the mainstream by starting to dress in a bohemian manner, wearing his hair long and by declaring himself to be an atheist.

He fell in love with Fanny Osbourne, a married woman with children, estranged from her husband, when he met her in 1876, and married her in 1880 in San Francisco. After his marriage, Stevenson started producing his best-known works: *Treasure Island* (1883), *Kidnapped* (1886) and *The Strange Case of Dr Jekyll* and *Mr Hyde* (1886).

He died of stroke on 3 December in 1894 at his home in Vailima, Samoa.

■ Characters

Dr Henry Jekyll: A respected doctor and a well-known altruist, Dr Jekyll struggles between his good self and the dark side of his personality which secretly engages in corrupt and lustful acts, and which he often represses. He compounds a chemical to separate this dark side of his nature from the dual personality he was born with.

Mr Edward Hyde: A strange, repulsive man who looks faintly pre-human. He is the form taken on by the dark side of Dr Jekyll's personality. Everyone feels he is deformed in some way though no one can say exactly why; he arouses a feeling of deep fear and disgust in anyone who looks at him. He is cruel, remorseless, lustful and violent.

Mr Gabriel John Utterson: A well-respected lawyer in London, an old friend of both Dr Jekyll and Dr Lanyon. He is an extremely loyal friend and an empathetic human being who is non-judgmental and tolerant of the faults of others.

Dr Hastie Lanyon: A reputed doctor in London and an old friend of both Dr Jekyll and Mr Utterson. He is a hearty, healthy, dapper gentleman with a decided manner. His rationalism and skepticism contrast with the mysticism of Dr Jekyll's chosen path. He is the first person to witness the transformation of Hyde into Jekyll and never recovers from this shock.

Mr Poole: Mr Poole is Dr Jekyll's butler for twenty years. His concern that his master might have been murdered by Mr Hyde leads him to seek Mr Utterson's help.

Mr Richard Enfield: Mr Enfield is a distant cousin and friend of Mr Utterson, with whom he regularly goes on walks on Sundays. Both of them are reserved men. Mr Enfield is a person who stands up for the right cause.

Mr Guest: Mr Guest is Mr Utterson's clerk and confidant, a man whose opinion he values. He is also an expert in analyzing handwriting.

Sir Danvers Carew: Sir Carew is a Member of Parliament, an aged gentleman with a good reputation. He is brutally beaten to death one night by Mr Hyde. He is also a client of Mr Utterson.

Inspector Newcomen: An inspector from Scotland Yard who is in charge of investigating the murder of Sir Danvers Carew.

■ Questions

Chapter 1
- *What kind of a person was Mr Utterson?*
- *Why was the Blackmail House called so?*

Chapter 2
- *Why did Dr Jekyll's will disturb Mr Utterson?*
- *Why did Mr Utterson visit Dr Lanyon?*

Chapter 3
- *Describe Mr Hyde.*
- *How did Dr Jekyll defend his protégé and what does he make Utterson promise?*

Chapter 4
- *Describe Sir Danvers Carew's murder.*
- *What evidence of Hyde's guilt did Mr Utterson and Inspector Newcomen find on searching his house in Soho?*

Chapter 5
- *What did Mr Utterson's conclude after reading the letter entrusted to him by Dr Jekyll?*
- *What did Mr Guest say about Hyde's handwriting that unnerved Mr Utterson further?*

Chapter 6
- *How had Dr Jekyll changed after Hyde's disappearance?*
- *Describe Dr Lanyon's changed appearance.*

Chapter 7
- *Why did Poole pay Mr Utterson a sudden visit?*
- *What was Mr Utterson's response to Poole's request?*

Chapter 8
- *What was Mr Utterson's initial interpretation of Poole's account of the masked figure?*
- *How did Poole convince him that the creature was not Dr Jekyll but Hyde?*

Chapter 9
- *Describe what Poole and Mr Utterson find on breaking down the door to the room?*
- *Describe the contents of the envelope?*

Chapter 10
- *Describe the contents of the letter that Dr Lanyon received.*
- *What happened after Hyde drank the medicine?*

Chapter 11
- *Why did Dr Jekyll wish to separate the evil side of his personality from the good side?*
- *How did Dr Jekyll try to explain the reason behind Hyde being younger and shorter than himself?*

Chapter 12
- *How did the form of Hyde grant Dr Jekyll certain "strange immunities", both of his physical self as well as those of conscience?*
- *Why was it difficult for Dr Jekyll to make a final choice between the two selves?*

Chapter 13
- *Why did the medicine lose its efficacy?*
- *How did Jekyll's relationship with Hyde change over time?*